The Kiss of Dea

The Kiss of Death
By Sarah Natale

Kellan Publishing

Copyright © Sarah Natale
Front and back cover art by Peg Pappa
First Kellan Publishing: June 2015
www.kellanpublishing.com

The Kiss of Death
By Sarah Natale

Prologue
Messina, Sicily ~ October 1347

"*Leave,* go far away! You and your sailors have brought death and destruction to our city! Board your ships and be gone!"

~

Genoa, Italy ~ January 1348

"Papa! Papa! They're here!" a young boy shouted with excitement as three Genoese ships sailed into the Mediterranean harbor from Messina. His dark curls were whipped across his face as the wind picked up, sending a chill through his bones. But he didn't care. He loved watching his father unload trading ships and come home with treasures upon treasures galore. His father regarded him with a sigh and ruffled his hair.

"Ah, Nicholaus."

"What will it be this time, Papa?" the boy asked. A number of things popped into his head. Exotic spices, silks, jewels – the list went on and on.

"Patience, *bambino,*" said his father.

"Giuliano!" a male voice called to him. "Come quickly. They're almost ready!"

Giuliano turned to enter the docks, leaving his son with a warm look. He followed the other men, taking in the path and direction of the strong winds.

Always makes for a good trade day in the seaport, he thought.

There was plenty of work to be found unloading goods in this kind of weather. He stepped foot on the deck of one of the galley ships, marveling at his good fortune. It was roughly 200 feet long and propelled by heavy oars that required about 1,200 sailors to row. In his mind, this meant lots of expensive cargo. He was in luck. His muscles bulged with the weight of the crates as he lifted them easily with his strong arms, cradling them in his grasp as he bustled about. This was a man's work.

Beyond the dock, Nicholaus watched his father and fellow laborers work in awe, wishing he, too, was old enough to do something as productive and rewarding as they. The carts of goods being unloaded both fascinated and intrigued him, and he entertained himself with fantasies of what they held and the lands they came from. Who touched that silk last? Who procured those spices and jewels? It was a wonderment to his lively imagination.

Finally, Giuliano, tired and a few bags of coins richer, finished his work on the ships at last. He joined his son on the docks as they headed home with some of the workers that had assisted in unloading. Nicholaus joined their laughter and jokes, again wishing he was one of the men instead of an eight-year-old. He watched them amuse themselves, telling stories and picking fleas off their sleeves that had most likely come from the ships. One such story involved the spread of a mysterious disease carried by a poisonous cloud from the East. The men laughed at the absurd tale, agreeing that it was too far away to affect them, if it were even true. Soon the stories turned to happier tales and suggestions of what they should do with their newly earned wages.

It was a productive day.

The next morning, upon coming down to breakfast to

greet his father, Nicholaus realized that he was nowhere to be found. His mother told him that he was ill and in bed and would not be coming to breakfast today. Sad and sulky, Nicholaus settled down to breakfast by himself. He loved his father and especially loved spending time with him. He was supposed to help him learn to fish today. Surely, he couldn't be sick.

"I'm sorry, *bambino*," his mother said. "He will be well to take you fishing soon."

"Jacobella . . ." came a low, raspy voice, sounding as though it took much effort to utter those four syllables.

"He needs me," she said. She kissed her son on the forehead and left to attend to her husband.

But, contrary to Jacobella's high hopes, Giuliano's condition did not improve. She received word from the wives of the men who had helped unload ships yesterday that some were found dead in their beds this morning. Gossip claimed that the three ships that had arrived in the seaport had within two days affected every inch of the city. The sailors and citizens alike were falling ill, some dying immediately. She thanked the Lord that Giuliano only had a slight fever. But, he just kept getting worse: fever, chills, swelling of the glands. She wanted to help, but there was nothing she could do. His condition grew more and more severe with the progression of days. Time seemed to stop for everyone in the house.

By the third day, cries from the *becchini* could be heard from the streets, coming to carry away the dead. She averted her eyes when going out to the market and tried to avoid the stench of the carts of bodies. But, the next day, Giuliano was no better. Jacobella hugged Nicholaus close to her bosom as he cried and cried endlessly. Rumors were all over the city about an unseen, but deadly illness from the ships. The family feared they would all soon meet the same fate as their beloved husband and father.

There was no escape.

Chapter One

London, England ~ November 1, 1348

"Matthias, you really know how to make a person lose her insides," I said, clutching my sides. It was astounding that it wasn't the play we were seeing, *The Pride of Life*, that was making me laugh so hard, but the person I was here with. Albeit an absurd comment, but funny just the same.

"Elizabeth."

"You scoundrel. That was *not* the King's intention. That was his messenger, Mirth. Think before you –"

"Elizabeth."

"What?"

"You – nothing."

"No, tell me."

"That was most certainly his intention," Matthias said quite frankly. "The King of Life was too busy relying on his bodyguards, Health and Strength, which was why he challenged Death to a fight. Death will ultimately win, for one cannot mess with one of the Seven Deadly Sins and expect to escape punishment. It's a breach of morality. And the King's sin is pride."

"Yes, I can see that, the play is based upon morals, but you don't have to be so rude –"

"Rude? Me? I was only explaining –"

All this talk of sin brought up a good question. "Matthias, let me ask you, have you been to service today?" I said, cutting him off from whatever secondary joke he was about to make.

"Well, it *is* the Feast of All Saints," he told me, as if I didn't already know that.

"Precisely."

"And? I paid my dues to the Lord. Can't a fellow have a little humour if he so pleases?"

"That was not 'a little humour,' that was a –"

"All right, all right, we shall bet on it, yes?"

I rolled my eyes.

"Cross and pile. I'll even give you first pick." He pulled a coin out of his outside kirtle pocket. One side held a cross and the other a familiar countenance of a man's face. It seemed to call to me, beckoning me to choose: cross or pile?

I shrugged. "Pile."

"It's settled then. Pile: you're right. Cross: I'm right. Here I go." He flicked his wrist and the coin did a somersault in the air before landing back in the palm of his hand. The familiar coin face stared back at me. "It's pile. You lose."

"How dare you! I won fairly and you know it! Give me that traitorous coin!" I grappled for his hand.

"Shhh!" someone in the audience shrieked.

I gave Matthias a look, but he just smiled to himself in silence for the duration of the performance. I sighed in exasperation. He knew I couldn't stay angry at him for long. And I knew he was just trying to irritate me enough to get into a row with him. He didn't really mean anything by it. We were childhood friends, at each other's throats all the time. We knew and loved each other like family. Nothing could come between us, not even foolish bickering. He was apprenticed to my father's shop, after all.

My father, Paul Chauncey, was the successful, proud and wealthy owner of the Chauncey craftsman shop. He had owned it for years and had been renting the upper rooms out to tenants for as long as I could remember. That was where the majority of his income came from. Most craftsmen lived in the townhouse they set up shop in, but not my father. He was the proud exception. And, most craftsmen weren't wealthy either, but my father was as good as nobility around here. He was known for his quality work.

Now, we were not a family of nobles by any means, but we lived in a manor house just the same. My father was just that successful. The Chauncey family was actually a distant relative to the noble family of de Lacy, but I had never met them in all my years. To us, it was as if they didn't exist. For all purposes we neither lived nor acted like nobility, and we certainly were not anything like that of our distant relatives. We did not take part in Lord and Lady rituals or have titles like Duke or Duchess, Princess or Squire, Count or Countess, or anything like that. What the de Lacys did was of no concern to us. We just lived in a fancy house and had fancy servants. In other words: we lived with all the amenities of a noble family, minus the snobbery.

In my opinion, it was my father's dedication and

hard work that helped him become successful, but our nobility ties that gave him the resources to get started. And I respected him for that. Many rich-by-blood families would just sit on their money and squander it until there was nothing left.

Not my father. He invested it. He took care of us. He loved us.

And I loved him so much.

When the play ended, Matthias and I went our separate ways, but not before he made it perfectly clear that he had been right from the beginning. He was gloating the entire time we exited the theatre.

"Fine, I will admit that the King of Life *was* conquered by Death after all," I said at last. But what Matthias was forgetting was that I was right too: the King's life was not lost to death – his soul survived. It was saved from the fiends by intercession from Our Lady. And I told him as much.

"Details, details," Matthias mused. "I will not concern myself with such trivial matters." I sighed, an action that abruptly turned to laughter as Matthias again proceeded to make a joke out of the whole matter. This time I just let the laughter sink in instead of arguing with him.

It was supper time, and I just made it home in time. I made sure to first wash my hands and face in my chamber with Saracen soap – the more expensive and luxurious kind because it was made with olive oil instead of sheep's tallow and scented with pine leaves. I tilted the water jug over my hands and rinsed them in the basin before drying them with a silk towel. I now felt fresh and clean – an appropriate image in which to come to supper. It was of great importance to wash one's hands before beginning a meal and considered rude to not do so, but a full body wash was not necessary. Bathing in our house did not occur very frequently because it required a lot of time and energy to heat the water for the bath, though we had servants to assist us in the process. I assumed it was even less frequent in peasant homes, since they didn't have servants or wooden tubs, and the firewood necessary to heat the water was often more expensive as winter approached.

Confident that I was ready to make an appearance, I strode into the dining hall and took a seat at the elaborate table before me as Cecily and Rohesia, our cook and highest servant, stood in the background. Rohesia began serving the first course of bread, cheese, and soup, while Cecily poured each of us a healthy glass of ale before disappearing into the kitchen to prepare the next course. My family, all five of us – my younger brother Josef, thirteen; younger sister Carrie, seven; *Moder*; *Fader*; and myself – began drinking our ale and engaging in polite conversation. The hearty drink was a staple and considered the healthiest refreshment you could put into your body, regardless of your age. And of course, it was only polite to discuss the events of the day, glass in hand.

"Pray tell me, what events did you take part in after service, Elizabeth?" my father asked me. We attended church services at St. Paul's Cathedral every week as a family. After that requirement was met, we could do as we pleased the rest of the day. I personally liked the service, but sometimes my younger siblings complained. Although I didn't see why. Our father trusted us with this mobility and freedom to do what we wanted; the least we could do was follow his rules and give grace to God first.

"I saw *The Pride of Life* with Matthias," I informed the table. Another rule of our family meals: everyone partook in conversation by adding to or at least listening to the words of those around them, so everyone generally knew the happenings of everyone else. Nothing was considered secret.

"Ah, yes, Matthias de Bourgueville. A respectable fellow. Nineteen years old and becoming more like a man every day," my father marveled. The Chaunceys and de Bourguevilles had been family friends for years. We were all quite close and often attended family celebrations together. "He will make a gracious maiden very proud someday."

I nodded, not sure what to say or how my father would take it if I voiced the thoughts I really felt. Instead, I kept them to myself and remained silent.

"How is the lad?" he pondered. "Tell him I need a new stock of oak chairs and linens this week. Juliana wants to do some seam work to add to the shelves."

I nodded again. Conversation ensued like that, with Juliana – my mother – and Carrie adding bits and pieces here and there. *Moder* often had her own conversations with the younger children, whereas I, the oldest, took part in more adult topics with my father. Which I didn't mind in the least bit. I was sixteen. Responsibility suited me well.

The second course of the meal consisted of beef flavoured with a sauce of leeks, garlic, and herbs. The third, or *desert*, much to Carrie's delight, consisted of sugar conserves. A delicacy. Filled and satisfied, we retired to our respective chambers for the night.

The next morning, breakfast was a little bit delayed. "Cook is sick," Rohesia told me. She lowered her voice to a whisper, so as not to upset the other children. "We fear it may be *influenza*." And it was a legitimate fear indeed. Once a person contracted the dreaded influenza, it often meant they were in for the worst. Severe fevers followed by swift death often ensued. And our cook, Cecily, had a very high fever. I sent her a silent prayer from my heart.

Household events did not change much; Rohesia filled in for a lot of Cook's duties. Meals went on as usual. But by the third day, I could tell something was very wrong. No one came down to breakfast, and not one of the beds was made. *What is the problem with our servants today?* I wondered. I wandered around the house in search of family or servant when I heard a sharp cry from Cecily's chamber. At once I picked up speed and entered the servant hallway. I stood in the hall's doorway to see what was the matter. *Moder* and *Fader* were there, stone-faced, *Moder* hiding the children behind her and Rohesia sitting in a corner, hands covering her face, weeping. I was afraid to look. But something made me do so anyway. I crept closer to the chamber entrance. There on the bed Cecily lie, perfectly still and pale, hands at her sides. I turned away. *Moder* didn't even have to ask me to take my siblings' hands and escort them away from the room. I did so instinctively.

Chapter Two

The next morning, Rohesia entered my room as usual to wake me and help me dress for my day. Everything was back to normal. No one mentioned the events from yesterday. The servant girl's face was cheery and lively, all evidence of the tears from yesterday completely gone with a smile replacing them in their wake. She helped me out of my sleepwear and handed me my undergarments: hose stockings and smock. The men's smock was called a shirt, but men wore hose over their legs the same as women. I slipped the hose on and she secured it at the knees with garters.

"Which over-garment would you like to wear today, ma'am?" she asked, holding up a warm, twill weave kirtle and cooler, silk kirtle. The kirtle, really just a long tunic, was my favourite article of clothing with its bold, bright colours and variety of styles. Lighter colours were worn more by the peasants, and envy them their clothing was something I never did. I loved indulging in fashion but immediately felt guilty for my vanity. I never compared myself to the less fortunate, whether to feel pity or superiority. It was just rude. What was with me today?

I instead busied myself with thoughts of the matter at hand by examining the kirtles laid out on the bed before me. Both materials were nice. The twill was heavier and warmer, but the silk was more comfortable and felt fine under the touch of my fingertips.

"Rather, are you planning to be outdoors today?" the servant rephrased.

I was. I wanted to make an errand. I glanced outside at the steady, cool November rain casting the streets. "Better go with the twill," I said.

As she assisted me with my clothing, her lively chatter put me at ease and kept my thoughts from wandering to last night. Oftentimes her mindless chatter was a bit annoying, but today I welcomed it as something of the norm to ground my thoughts. Mindless or not, it served as a distraction. And she obviously shared my love of fashion. "Oh, how I love dressing nobility!" she squealed. "Kirtles, mantles, gowns, hoods, surcoats! It's all so *fun*!"

I didn't bother reminding her that we weren't really nobility. Just well-off.

For outerwear I pulled a shorter over-kirtle on top of the longer twill one, and Rohesia finished the look with a belt, brooch, and surcoat lined with fur for warmth before handing me my gloves. "Have a good day, ma'am," she said.

Outside the streets were a nightmare. Nothing particularly abnormal of a typical November day, but irritating just the same. The streets were already crowded and narrow, scarcely wide enough for a horse, human, or the occasional cart, let alone the muck created from this horrible weather. The downpour of rain only added to the mêlée. My shoes made an odd squeaking sound from the suction as the dirt from the unpaved streets slowly turned to a soupy mess of mud. At least the foul smell of the streets from hot summer days would be somewhat alleviated with the arrival of winter, which would be any day now.

I *squeak squawked* down the street until I got to my father's shop, thankful it was only a short walk from the manor house. It was all but empty. Matthias didn't have work today, and I assumed *Fader* was in back restocking as the only customer was little Carrie. She often liked to spend time in the store with him as he worked. The sights and sounds of customers in a busy shop intrigued her. I

13

think she wanted to grow up to be just like *Fader*. I didn't blame her. It had to be an exciting job. Although, I'd never heard of a woman working a craftsman shop before and didn't want to be the one to break the news to her. *Fader's* legacy would probably be passed down to Josef when he came of age, if he accepted. We were all pretty sure that he would. Either him or Matthias.

"Lizzie!" Carrie called, seeing me enter. She skipped over to me. "Where's Matty?"

"He doesn't work today," I said, patting her on the head. She hugged me and motioned for me to join her by the toy section. I tried to pay attention as she showed me the brand-new children's section she had helped *Fader* design, something she was very proud of indeed, but her mention of Matty had brought him to the forefront of my mind, and I couldn't help thinking about him. I was kind of hoping I would run into him today, although logic told me that I wouldn't. He never worked on Thursdays: family matters. I was also kind of hoping we could make up with each other after the bickering incident we had had at the showing of *The Pride of Life*, which had been both slightly embarrassing but somehow humourous. Not that he held anything against me for it, which he surely didn't. And I didn't think any less of him even though I had acted like I did, and he knew that, too. It was a silly worry, really. Quite nonsensical if I thought about it. I just didn't want any bad blood between us. We were too close for that.

Although, every essence of my being secretly wished that we could be closer, somehow. It was foolish, I knew, but I desired it just the same. How I wished it were possible to court Matthias! I found myself fantasizing about it all the time. Too much, actually. Definitely more than a sane human being should. We were close, close enough to

14

be brother and sister – that's how deep our family-friends tie went. But somehow, that wasn't enough for me. I wanted to be close like a husband and wife. To share not only our thoughts and feelings, but our goals and hopes and desires . . . and to one day make a family together . . . Matthias would make a good father. I was sure of that. He was handsome and kind and courteous – *Fader* was right when he said that he was well on his way to becoming a respectable young man. In my opinion, he already was. He was everything I had always wanted and everything I could never have. My parents would never allow it. Maybe his would, but that was such an off-putting thought that there was no sense in even considering it. And say they did allow it, well, what would I do if he didn't feel the same?

"Lizzie, what are you doing?"

"Hmm?" My sister's voice snapped me out of my reverie.

"You were planning something, I know you were," she said. Clever, observant girl, she was. "I saw your thoughts dancing around in your head."

"Oh, nothing really, Carrie," I said. "Just a fantasy that can never happen."

This unintentionally intrigued her. "Ooh, fantasy? Like in fairy tales? Tell me, tell me!" she squealed.

I sighed. What was the harm in telling my little sister? She would probably only see it as a joke, which was just as well. It was all a joke anyway. I was fooling myself every time I thought about it. "Ah, Carrie, you silly girl. Just imagining what it would be like to court Matthias, that's all."

"Oh, Lizzie," she said, her eyes suddenly very intrigued by the texture of the wooden floor, as if she were afraid to meet my gaze. She was substantially less enthusiastic than I thought she would be. In fact, her previous enthusiasm dropped about two notches at the mention of my fantasized betrothal. Thankfully, she went on before I even had to ask. "You can't . . ."

"I know I can't. It's just a fantasy, like I said."

"No, you don't know," she went on, looking like she was almost in tears. "*Moder* and *Fader* already have plans for you to wed shortly. I – I remember hearing them speak about it late one night when I couldn't sleep. What a shame: 'Lizzie and Matty can't be betrothed.'"

My eyes popped out of my head. "They said that!?" I mean, I knew they would never allow it, but still. That was always just a speculation.

"No, *I* said that. But it's the same thing," she sniffled. "Oh, Lizzie, it's so sad! You and Matty are perfect together! You should get married! I want you to." She latched her arms around my torso, holding me tight. I waved away her supportive qualms in favor of receiving more information. This was an unplanned for complication.

"Did they say who I was to marry?"

"No, I don't think so," she sighed. "Just that they want you to. And soon. All the noble girls marry at twelve or fourteen, you know. And you've been sixteen for a while."

How dare they! We were not noble in the least bit! I didn't care how old my second cousin twice removed was when she got married! I didn't care how much of a harlot she was. I refused to be like the de Lacys! Now, I didn't have a problem with this sudden interest in my marriage plans if it was someone with whom I would actually want to spend the rest of my life. In fact, I would welcome the idea. I had fancied Matthias since I was very young. But chances were that my betrothal would probably end up being someone I had never met before. And the fact that my parents would want to resort to arranged marriage when we were hardly even related to the nobles, well, that to me was absurd. But the longer I mulled over it, the more I realized that *I* was the one being absurd. Of course they would arrange a marriage. Why wouldn't they? I was the oldest, after all. It was the easiest way to ensure the monetary value of our family remained in our family.

And I knew it was uncommon to marry for love amoungst nobility. In fact, many of them scorned the idea of love and refused to believe that it even existed among married couples. Courtly love with unseen squires and knights, maybe, but that was kept under wraps and such scandals were rarely reported, thought they undoubtedly happened. But love or not, I refused to consider myself nobility. I suddenly wished I was a peasant girl, growing up in an impoverished home without the amenities of fashion or even substantial food on the table, all so I could love who I wanted, marry who I wanted, live how I want-ed.

"Poor Lizzie," my sister squeaked, and to my sur-prise promptly began to do my crying for me while I stood in shocked submission. "I'm sorry," she whispered be-tween sobs. I was surprised at how comforted I felt by her concern. *The best comfort in the world comes from a seven-year-old*, I thought, amused. Still, the fact that she saw nothing wrong with my fancying someone I could never have, well, maybe that meant I hadn't gone mad. Or may-be she had gone mad, too.

Maybe I was only just slightly mad. I could live with that.

Still, I felt my heart drop in my stomach as I accepted my fate. I had known from the start I would never be allowed to marry Matthias. He needed to be able to support himself financially first; those were the rules. This was no shock to me. So why did I feel so crushed inside?

Chapter Three

The next morning I awoke to the sound of a high-pitched scream. I jumped out of bed and had just opened my chamber door when my mother came dashing into my room. I almost ran smack into her. I heard *Fader* shouting down the hall: "Juliana! JULIANA, what's *WRONG*!" but she didn't budge from her spot near my door. I read the expression on her face and knew what had happened before she even uttered a word: the servant was dead.

I later learned of the details. She was perfectly healthy yesterday morning. Now she had dropped dead like a fly, without so much as a cough or fever to give away the cause of her illness. It was the second death in the Chauncey house. Poor Rohesia . . .

Rumors spread rapidly as we heard that ours was not the only house afflicted with this fast-moving plague. And a plague it was, for there was no better name for this mysterious disease that seemed to infect everyone it came into contact with. It was all over the city, and not just in London, either. It was spreading rapidly all over Europe. There were stories of this very illness in Italy, France, and Spain. The horrors of it were not to be taken lightly. Some said it originated in Italy; others claimed it came from as far away as the Far East, carried by a poisonous cloud.

Soon, all social gatherings were cancelled, including Sunday service, since "large gatherings of persons in compact spaces pose a threat to the citizens' health," as per the words of the Alderman of London in his speech on Wednesday. Carrie and Josef were not all that upset at this development, but I felt a certain sadness at seeing St. Paul's Cathedral close its doors to the people. It was as though a part of me became closed with it, and I couldn't shake the odd sense of doom that seemed to seep into my veins as the enormity of the situation washed over me. The closing of churches had the ability of making this catastrophe very real in a way that nothing else could. If you didn't have your connection to God, you had nothing. And I felt very unsteady. Could it be that God was punishing us lowly sinners with this strange, evil disease?

I guess I shouldn't have been surprised when my brother Josef took sick next. The disease was everywhere and it was inevitable that it would reach our house again, seeing as our manor was already exposed due to the deaths of both our cook and our highest servant. The two women had most likely died of the disease. The doctor said it was safe to assume that any sudden death after the first of November was due to this mysterious plague. This statement was meant to encourage extra awareness and precaution against the disease so we could halt its spread, though that gave me no more comfort than saying that Cook really had died of influenza after all. In an odd, sick, twisted way, I felt like I would feel better if it *had* been influenza.

It was an atrocity. All of it. I felt like I would lose my mind if I stayed in that house another minute. So when *Moder* gave me orders to fetch the doctor, I gladly obliged. The rush of fresh air would do me some good, she had said.

Unfortunately, the air outside was no more fresh or inviting than that inside our house. The stench of dead and decaying bodies was overwhelming, and I covered my nose in my kerchief. I had my head down the entire time to avoid the gaze of the infected on the streets and was about a block from the doctor's when I stumbled headlong into Matthias.

"Aargh!"

"Elizabeth?"

"Good heavens, Matty, you scared me half to death."

"Might I remind you that it was *you*, fair madam, who collided into *me*."

"You mustn't humour me with flattery," I scolded him, though my heartbeat betrayed me by speeding up ever so slightly with the idea that he thought me "fair."

"Mustn't I?" He grinned that beautiful grin I knew so well.

"Matthias," I said. His smile made me melt. I again found myself vaguely wishing he would ask me to marry him. And again, all the same qualms from before flooded my memory. He was too young; he needed to build up a craftsman career to support himself before he could even think about building and supporting a family, et cetera, et cetera.

He took my arm and pulled me to the side of the street. Every nerve ending in my arm was on fire at his touch, and when I looked up, the seriousness of his expression caught me off guard. Suddenly he was all business. "Listen, Lizzie," he said. "You were on your way to the doctor's I take it?" He didn't even give me a chance to respond. "Meaning you probably know that this illness is serious stuff. But I doubt you know how serious."

His mouth was a tight line. I waited for him to continue.

"My brother just died from it."

"Oh, Matty," I cried. My heart ached over his loss.

We had only lost a few of our servants. The loss of a family member was an entirely different matter. I wrapped my arms around him and held him close, the ache of his misfortune making me forget how odd I would feel being this close to him under any other circumstances. "Do they know how it is transmitted?"

"Some doctors say through contact with the swelling buboes, others say you will drop dead if you even breathe the same air as a victim."

"Well, I know that one is false," I informed him. "My entire manor has to be infected since both Cook and Rohesia have passed, and now my brother has it. But the rest of us are in good health. Fit as ever. It must be through direct contact."

"Maybe," was all he said. His expression was dark and unreadable, and that scared me the most. I could always tell what he was thinking without a second thought, and now I couldn't even tell if he believed me or not. I wrote it off as grief over his brother and plunged on to something less taxing on the body and soul.

"St. Paul's Cathedral is closed. Did you hear? No more service until, well, indefinitely, I guess. Until this plague is over."

"Ah, I'm sure you and your family are very distraught." He himself didn't look too distraught about it.

"Matthias, what's the matter with you? Don't you believe in God anymore?" I scolded. "Of course you do what am I saying?"

He looked me dead in the eye. "What kind of God would do this to us, Elizabeth? How could He, who loves us so much, inflict such pain and cruelty? Think about it."

"I think He just needs to punish the sinners – as bad as it sounds, He just needs to wipe a few of them off this Earth. Kind of like *Noah and the Ark*. I think it's the same concept."

"But everyone is getting it. Everyone is being punished? Everyone's a sinner?" His green eyes bore into mine, searching my soul. Testing me.

"Well, technically, everyone *is* a sinner. Even the pastors admit as much." I could tell immediately afterward that this was not the response he wanted. Matthias was becoming cold to me, someone I didn't know anymore. And without him, and without God, I didn't know who or what to trust anymore. My instincts? Or the death and destruction before my eyes all around me . . . ?

"If everyone is a sinner, everyone dies. That's what you're saying. You're essentially giving us all a death sentence, Elizabeth. Is that really what you want? You're saying the entire world has to be cleansed. Until when? Until there's no one left?"

"Maybe it just needs to be cleansed of people like you: disbelievers." It was out of my mouth before I could rephrase it. I couldn't take it back. I felt pity on him, sure, that suffering could make him turn away from God like that, but there was no excuse for my words. I saw the fear and hurt in his eyes. Fear of the disease, of his brother's death, of God. And hurt from me and God alike. Guilt immediately sunk into my bones. I wished to God I could take it all back. But Matthias, the strong man that he was, didn't let it show how hard my words had hit him.

"Elizabeth," he said simply. "I don't want to argue.

Whatever your religious views, I know that in this time of need, we need to stick together – we need each other."

A silence passed between us, and in that silence it was neither awkward nor strained. I knew I was forgiven. Just like that.

"Have you heard the stories?" I inquired, hoping to create a brighter mood. I saw his eyes lighten with interest. Thank goodness my old Matthias was back. "You know, about a poisonous cloud come to kill us all or some such thing."

"The cloud from the Far East, of course," he said, and immediately slipped into story mode, something he was amazing at. "The story goes that there was a horrible war between the sea and the sun in the Indian Ocean a couple years ago, and in rebellion, the waters of the ocean were pulled up into the sky in a cloud of vapor. The vapor contained dead and rotting fish, causing a stench so bad, people died at its scent. The sun could not consume this terrible vapor, nor could the vapor fall back to the Earth as rain, so it continues to drift over the ocean causing illness and suffering to all the ships and sailors it meets. Hence the infected ships in Italy who first brought this plague to Europe."

"Is it true?" I whispered.

"Who knows? I'd trust Doc most if I were you. He knows his trade."

"Yes, I must have a word with him soon."

"Well, I mustn't keep you."

"Take care, Matthias. I'll pray for your brother."

He didn't say anything to that as I turned and headed in the direction I had originally been going. Once I fetched the physician, we hurried back to the manor. He hovered over my brother's bed as he administered whatever cure he saw fit.

Chapter Four

The first thing I noticed about him was that he was dressed in the strangest getup I had ever seen. He wore elaborate layers of clothing, complete with a long, dark robe and pointed hood. He said it was meant to keep away the disease. Attached to the hood was a mask with a long, pointed nose which much resembled a bird's beak and which he told us contained vinegar and herbs to cover the "smell of death." It also had the pungent odor of various perfumes which were so strong I could hardly tell how he could stand it. He said it worked wonders in preventing him from both smelling the stench of open buboes and from breathing "contaminated air." Phrases like "diseased air" came up a lot in conversation with him. So I guess Doc believed in Matthias's theory of contamination by breathing. That one I could actually believe and couldn't blame him for his strange attire: how could one smell *anything* with that awful smell covering his nose? It had to block out every stench in the vicinity. But I guess, being a doctor, he had to encounter a lot of smelly patients. And judging from the aromas of the sick outside in the streets, they couldn't be good.

He also was adorned in leather gloves and heavy boots, and it was the most bizarre and gruesome sight I had ever seen. To complete the look of terror, he wore an amulet of dried blood and ground-up toads at his waist, for good luck, I guess. I had never believed in superstitions myself, but after seeing the death in the streets all around me, I was willing to try. He also explained that in addition to the perfumes and vinegar in his "beak" (he didn't call it a beak but I found it quite humourous to not call it anything but), he doused himself with vinegar and chewed angelica before approaching any victim. That also helped explain, in part, his awful smell. That coupled with the overwhelming perfumes, and whew, he was quite a character to behold. The spectacle he created of himself certainly terrified me when I first laid eyes on him.

And if it offered him the protection necessary to be here right now to speed my brother's recovery, I couldn't complain. Josef had dark, black buboes covering what seemed like every inch of his skin – something neither Rohesia nor Cecily had had. The doctor couldn't explain why that was, though he said it was not uncommon for a victim of the plague to experience no symptoms at all and be perfectly healthy one minute and completely lifeless by morning. I shivered, remembering with scary clarity how normal Rohesia had seemed, and then, just like that, she was *gone*. Not one symptom to give a reason for her absence from the world. It made me cringe viscerally.

The physician examined Jo's buboes, which were originally small pustules that seemed to grow bigger every day. First they were the size of walnuts; now they much resembled hen eggs and were soon approaching the size of goose eggs. We told him as much and he said that was quite normal for the disease. Not good, just normal. Well, I'd be darned if anything was considered normal these days. I didn't know right from left anymore. My entire world was flipped upside down the day Cecily up and died on us.

In addition to physical maladies, poor Josef also suffered from intense headaches and chills following a fever that turned right back into fever again. There was nothing we could do to alleviate his pain. He complained that he was constantly nauseous and would vomit back up everything we fed to him. Sometimes the vomit was red with blood. And sometimes he would utter strange words that made no sense to us, to the point where we were sure he was seeing things that were not there. The doctor said that these types of hallucinations often happened and were usually in conjunction with violent deliriums. Well, that explained the crazy behaviour of the afflicted outside. You would think they had gone mad. And, I guess with a disease as horrible as that, they had.

In addition to all these ailments, Josef often complained of stiff pain in his arms, legs, and back, and that the horrible, black swellings all over his body – mainly on his neck, under arms, and inner thighs – were hard and painful. I took pity on him. No child anywhere should have to experience such malaise.

"I am to examine the face, hands, eyes, posture, breathing, sleep, stool, urine, vomit, and sputum of the patient," the doctor said by way of explanation for his actions. "That is the best way to get a good sense of his bodily humours: phlegm, blood, yellow bile, and black bile. These four humours make up the human body and are associated with qualities of hot, cold, moist, and dry. Disease is caused by an excess of a humour, and one can treat this condition by changing the body's heat to moisture ratio." We listened intently as he schooled us in the latest in medical knowledge of the inner workings of the human body.

A time passed. Everyone in the house was ill at ease as the doctor did his work to confirm whether this was indeed the dreaded plague, or by some hopeful chance anything, literally *anything* else. Finally, at long last, he cleared his throat.

"Yes?" said *Moder*.

"Finished at last, my dear Juliana."

"Is it . . . ?" I couldn't bring myself to finish my sentence.

"It is indeed the Great Pestilence, I am heartily sorry to say. What a shame, a boy of only thirteen years. Still, younger than he have died horrible deaths to this disease."

He obviously was not helping matters with this kind of commentary. Seeming to read my mind, and as eager to move on from the negatives and get on with the cure as I was, *Moder* pressed, "What is your prescription, Doctor?"

"For the head pains try sweet-smelling herbs: rose, lavender, or sage will do. For the chronic stomach pain and sickness: wormwood, mint, or balm should do the trick. He doesn't seem to have problems with his breathing or lungs like some of the others, otherwise licorice and comfrey would see to that. Douse everything in vinegar to halt the spread of the disease. And before I go, I will administer the best form of treatment to speed recovery. A good bleeding will help rid the body of some of the bad blood in his system. And whatever you do, *do not bathe*. Neither him nor anyone in these times should submerge thyself in bath water, for it will further the spread of the disease from contact with the skin. That is the most dangerous thing you can do." I was secretly thankful I hadn't bathed in over a month. "And for the unaffected, in order to maintain your peak health, take these precautions: the disease is sometimes transmitted through air due to the awful smell put out from the dead and dying, so if you must go outside, use a handkerchief to cover your face, and dip it in some aromatic oil. It will do you well." I gave an internal leap for joy: I already did this! "There are also some talismans that former patients have said show success in warding off the disease, but I do not market these, nor do I sell them. However, if these interest you, I may direct you to someone who does. I must warn though, some are quite expensive.

"And finally, incense, incense, *incense*. I cannot tell

you how good of a job that has done for me in warding off the smell. Use whatever you have, buy more, it does not matter. Both myself and successful patients have used a number of scents: juniper, laurel, pine, rosemary, even sulfur."

"How about lemon leaves?" I asked. We had plenty of those in the kitchen which we used as flavouring for teas.

"Those work too!"

And now the dreaded question: the recovery rate. Rather, what were Josef's, specifically, chances for recovery? The physician told us that it was unclear as to Josef's survival, however if we implemented his techniques timely and correctly, we would see a break in his fever and he should soon reach recovery. It was indeed possible to recover from this malady. And that was all we needed to know.

Before leaving, the doctor gave him what he called a necessary "good bleeding," and I don't know why I stuck around to watch. It was a gruesome sight, more so than that of the physician, if that were possible. He cut open the vein nearest to his underarm, the most affected part of his body, and the blood that poured out was thick, black, and vile-looking, with a layer of green scum in it. It looked like, well, diseased blood. We thanked the doctor and he left to help his next patient. Though we appreciated his service, we were all secretly glad when he did. His visit was quite disturbing and at the very least, unnerving to the mind. We all prayed there was hope for Josef yet.

Chapter Five

Thankfully, I didn't have much time to think about it because within the hour I was sent back out to fetch some preventatives from the General Store, seeing as we were short on help and *Moder* said I was "quick and efficient" at it.

The death and disease covering the streets was worse, if that was even possible. People were running or jumping about frantically, not sure what to do because their mother, son, daughter, servant, or even they themself had caught the Great Mortality. It created quite a din in the already noisy London streets, and that was saying something. I heard the bells of St. Paul's Cathedral as I walked, and for a brief second felt a surge of hope as I registered that they were again reopening – everything was better now. But then my heart sank once more as I realized that the cathedral was no more open to the public than it had been before, and that a brave parson had simply gone in to start the ringing of the bells, which was often done in times of crisis, the plague being no exception. I heard a young couple on the street conversing that the bells were meant to drive the plague away. And I found myself thinking: *Well, whatever help*s.

The streets were not only cluttered with the living, but, as much as I hated to think of it, piles of the dead or dying as well. The stench of decaying bodies was ripe and foul-smelling, and at once I knew what the physician meant when he said smells were deadly. I pressed my handkerchief closer to my nose as I walked, passing several boarded up houses as I went. Plague Houses. I shuddered at the thought. I passed Smithfield Cemetery in Charterhouse Square where mass graves were taking shape; the undertakers – having run out of caskets, single grave plots, and time – had now hired men to pile the bodies into a mass grave instead. "Plague pits" as they were now called. It was disgusting. And utterly rude to the families of the dead. But I guess they did what had to be done. Still, I wished they would do something about the dead and decaying bodies still on the streets left to rot. People were dying rapidly. The death toll was increasing: at its height, 200 were buried each day.

I passed another disturbing scene of a band of about a dozen or so men strolling down the street whipping themselves and crying out that "the Lord forgive us all our trespasses." The Brotherhood of the Flagellants. I had heard of them but not actually seen them until now. I don't know how anyone else perceived them, but to me they were downright scary. They ignored me as I passed by, almost to the General Store now. Once there, I sought out an abundance of packets of incense and sweet-smelling herbs and even passed a quaint little sweetmeat shop on my way out. It featured a pretty decorative sign that read *Plague Preventatives Here: the Best Tested Cure*, and I thought, well, it couldn't hurt. They had taken the time to make the display so beautiful and pleasing to the eye. I vaguely wondered in the back of my mind if it was just a marketing ploy intending to take advantage of the people's trust in plague preventatives, but at the other end of my mind was the saying, "Desperate times call for desperate measures." And we could certainly use a little extra help in halting the spread of this disease, that much was clear. So, ploy or not, I purchased a few sweet goods in addition to my herbs and spices, and I was off.

I returned home with my packages at about half past nine, only to find a new disturbing change of events. Due to the documented cases of our servants becoming ill (I doubted they knew about my brother Josef having the disease yet), the law dictated that our house be shut up and everyone in it quarantined inside until further notice. My blood ran cold as I remembered the boarded up houses I had passed on my short errand. Only one thought registered in my mind to this development – which was essentially a death sentence – and that was the twisted motto: recover or die.

I knew how the stories went. A household member takes sick. Your house is boarded up. You contract the disease yourself due to the close quarters. You die. Everyone in the house dies. This was how entire families died. This was how many of our family friends had died. This was not how I wanted to die.

But there was nothing I could do. By morning our house, too, was shut up – sealed from the outside, locked and bolted so that no one could enter, but more importantly, no one could *leave*. It was a good preventative measure in the long run I guess, seeing as it kept the disease from spreading, that is if you didn't mind sacrificing a few entire families along the way. It only was truly awful if you were perfectly healthy, yet left to be trapped inside because the rest of your family was ill. As was the case with me. I was trapped inside a sick house that I could not escape, surrounded by a sick family I could not help, simply watching as more and more of my servants and family members took ill. Because there was nothing else I could do.

Hours passed, days. Nearly a week. I ate the preventative sweetmeats (and offered some to my family members before they became ill), hung incense everywhere, and basically lived in a cloud of smoky, ill-smelling incense holed up in my chamber. I prayed every night that God forgive us our sins, much like the ever-present Flagellants outside, and spare us. I prayed that my family recovered. I prayed that I survived. I prayed that Matthias survived, even if I never lived to see him again. Hired dead collectors could be heard up and down the streets every night shouting, "Bring out your dead!" incessantly over and over again until you felt as though your ears would bleed out the very words of death and destruction that were being hammered into your brain day in and day out. The men piled them into a cart several bodies high and carted them off to be dumped into the mass graves, sometimes five bodies deep. I knew this from the crack in the mortar in the back kitchen behind the stove. Through this tiny hole, I had a slight window to the world.

But it was not enough. There was nothing left to live for. Nothing. I began to scorn the fact that I was still perfectly well, all my faculties with me, for it meant that I had to endure an even bigger hell than the afflicted: being surrounded by the sick and dying with no way to save either them or myself and no way of knowing whether I would become them – no, that was inevitable. I rephrase. With no way of knowing *when* I would become them, the hour and day I would meet the same fate. It was torture. The torture of fear was the worst one cast to man by far. It could eat you alive, kill your spirit within you before you ever knew you had given up. And that, undoubtedly, that crash of spirit and life, led to the even more rapid spread of the disease. Those who were happy led longer lives always. That was the way.

And that would have been the end of me, I am sure, for I was on that route indefinitely. Until the day my mother gave me the best advice I had ever gotten. By now she was sick, too, and it was just me and Carrie left unscathed. I had outfitted the little one in a handkerchief and incense ensemble and had her hide out in her chamber the majority of the time, so I was sure she would stay safe and not wander into the dangerous parts of the house, like say, the sick parts, as children often did. I risked my own health by leaving the safe haven of my chamber once each day, going around the house to check on everyone. I was just outside my parents' chamber on one such occasion when I heard my mother stir. On her sickbed she could scarcely talk from all the coughing, but she whispered to me words that inspired me to keep on living.

"Eliz –" she choked. "Get out while you can, while you are still in good health. There is no hope left for us." She nodded to her condition. "But for you" – cough – "escape far, far away, and take the littlest –" cough, cough "– take your young sister, Carrie, with you –" cough, wheeze "– and always remember that I love you both." She smiled weakly.

"I love you, too, *Moder*," I whispered, grasping her hand tightly, well-aware that this would be our last meeting together. My lips formed over an unspoken *thank you* as her eyelids fluttered and closed and her breathing slowed. Then I did as I was told.

Chapter Six

I grabbed Carrie from her room where she was probably as bored as I had been (but probably not quite as ill in spirit), broke into my father's study/work area, stole a sledgehammer that belonged to his shop, and broke a hole in the back kitchen area behind the stove. I smashed the peephole through which was my only source of sunlight for the past interminable number of days and led Carrie through our back fence to the alleyways, the back way to the shop, so as not to be seen escaping a dreaded Plague House. I was sure we were not carrying the disease or we would have it by now, but anyone else would not be as sure. It was December now and extremely chilly outdoors. No one wanted to risk contagion. I wouldn't trust us either, if I were they.

We entered *Fader*'s shop through a secret hidden key under a board and I took no shame in ravaging it for anything we may need. It was musty and had the same shut-up feel our house had held, only minus the stigma of sickness. Obviously it had not been entered in some time, seeing as *Fader* had been out of commission for a while, what with being locked up in the Plague House and all. And Matthias had not been in here either, I thought with a sigh before immediately dismissing such foolish thoughts from my head. I took what we needed and left a few hours late through the store area, making sure to lock up shop before leaving, just in case of looters. They were running rampant these days, what with all the abandoned houses and buildings left vacant from the dead who did not need them anymore.

We were soon off, but not before I composed a letter to Matthias to make some last minute arrangements telling him of my staged breakout and plans to escape, and then passed it off to a young page boy. Matthias wrote back quickly and had the same boy deliver it under the door-mat to the shop. I saw him do so and immediately pulled it out from under the frost-bitten mat before it had a chance to freeze there. Matthias said in the letter that he would be happy to assist me, but that he could only go so far as the River Thames. For as much as he would have loved to come with us and escape this forsaken city to-gether, he must remain in London to help his family. I be-grudgingly agreed and was true on his offer to meet him near the bridge to the river.

My letter containing this final message would get there shortly, so all I had to do was make sure Carrie was ready to go. We stayed in the serenity of our father's shop for a little longer than we should have, both from a para-doxical effect of excitement and fatigue out of finally hav-ing escaped from that Plague House (I could no longer refer to it as our home), and simply reliving some comfort-ing memories of being in the shop where *Fader* worked. It was something forgotten and lost to us now – and some-thing we could never have or experience again. We must now move on, not look back, and consider ourselves lucky to be alive if we survived.

Since Carrie and I had staged our sneak out late last night, we were to meet at half past eleven in the morning. But before doing so I sent Carrie into the Sweet Shoppe to pick up a treat – anything she liked. I figured it would do her well. Matthias was to meet us a little ways down the street from the shop, near the River Thames.

I spotted him walking down the street from about a mile back, and the minute we laid eyes on each other, close enough to touch, he scooped me up into a giant hug.

"Elizabeth . . . ," he whispered, full of disbelief and astonishment. "You're alive." He hugged me even tighter, if that were possible, and I welcomed his embrace. I had to be as dumbfounded at seeing him as he was at seeing me. It was just so comforting to behold a friendly face.

"Of course I'm alive, Matty," I said.

"But you were shut up in that house for so long . . . everyone feared the worst –"

"You can say it," I said. Having looked death in the eye and survived, I no longer feared its presence as much as I once had.

"Well, Liz, we thought you and your entire family were dead."

My eyes teared up a little at that. "Josef is dead," I murmured. It was barely a whisper. "Died the second day we were shut up." A single tear slid down my face. "Matty, I – I'm sorry. I know now how you must have felt that day we got into that row, how it feels to lose a brother . . . and instead of comfort and support all you got was a religious bashing from me. Oh, I'm so sorry!"

"No, Elizabeth, I'm sorry. I was the one who was doubting God. He sent me one small challenge to see how I handled it, to test the strength of my faith, and I turned away from Him. Just when I needed Him most. I realized this the second you left, Liz. And I wanted you to know you were right all along . . ." He paused. "But you had already entered the doctor's office. And then your house was boarded up that night, and I never got a chance to see you again. Until now . . ." He looked at me like he was seeing me for the first time. "It wasn't until I thought I would lose you that I – I realized –"

And then he kissed me.

I felt as though an electric shock coursed through me as the fire of his kiss settled in my veins. It was like everything I'd ever imagined kissing him would be, and at the same time unlike anything I'd ever imagined. A part of me was secretly thrilled. But the other more rational part was screaming at me for my inappropriate reaction. I suddenly ripped myself away from him against my will, quickly but surely. It was one of the hardest things I'd ever done, besides break out of a Plague House, that is.

"What an abominable thing to do in a time of such illness!" I spat. "You could have it; I could have it? Who's to say we don't all have it and will have death beget us by sunset!" I was breathing heavily, both from the kiss and the outburst.

"Elizabeth," he said gently. "Listen to yourself." He grasped my arms, lightly but firmly.

"No." I struggled.

"I beseek you, cease your foolish talk and listen. If not to yourself, then to me."

I stopped my kicking and quieted myself, waiting for him to speak. Again, against my better judgment.

"Now, you don't know that," he began. "You have no right to speak those atrocities. Don't be nice and let such thoughts beset you. You're alive, and I'm alive. I'm a man of trade. I don't know a lot of things, but I know this. And one more thing: I know what my heart says. And if we both survive this hell, we shall be wed, regardless of what the parents say. Because Elizabeth, if this plague has taught me nothing other than one important lesson, it is this: life is too short to not live it fully. And if this is all the time I have left to live, I'd rather spend the rest of it with you."

"Ah, Matthias, I feel exactly the same way! However did you know!" And I pressed my lips against his before he could say another word. I knew now how tenuous our lives were and to treasure every precious second I had with him.

"If you guys are done making kissy faces," Carrie interrupted, "can we just get on with the wedding? I want to be the bridesmaid!" I had momentarily forgotten she was there and hoped we hadn't scared her. But she seemed more excited and intrigued by the idea of romance than anything else.

Matthias lifted an eyebrow. "A bridesmaid, eh?" The unspoken question rising in the face that I knew so well was ever clear to me: *She knows?*

"She has known for a while." I blushed. Seeming to take this as confirmation that he was right to confess his feelings to me as they were obviously mutual, he kissed me again. I didn't care who saw us there on the street or if the dead stood up in the graves to watch. If this was Hell - London and all the death and darkness around me – then this kiss with Matthias was my small piece of Heaven.

Chapter Seven

Carrie and I traveled the countryside for days until well into mid-December before we found a place to settle down. We holed up in the small town of Ardeley a little ways away from London, but miles upon miles on foot. It was a quaint, cute village, and the villagers all appeared healthy. We were welcomed warmly by a couple by the names of Favian and Seraphina Louvet. It was a peasant village – one could tell that just by looking at it – but the way those two beings held each other's gaze was unlike any I'd ever seen before. Even more than *Moder* and *Fader*, and I was sure they loved each other greatly, to a certain degree. But the Louvets were very much "in love," that much was clear. I envied them their simple peasantry way of life – free to love whomever they chose, and free to be with whomever they chose.

And then I remembered Matthias and our passionate kiss and how he had pledged his love to me, throwing caution to the wind about what any authority figure would think (namely his parents and mine) about the incident. No matter what anyone thought, I was his – as long as he would have me. And I think that was all that really mattered. As long as we mattered to each other, it would be enough. I saw it in Favian's eyes as he beheld Seraphina. And suddenly I did not feel envy or anger or any ill will toward them – instead I felt pride and joy. They had found love and let it survive and bloom. I could only hope it would be the same for Matty and me, that we could have that someday.

Village life was fairly simple, and Seraphina helped instruct me in the ways of cooking and cleaning and keeping a household going – things I had always had servants to do for me. It wasn't difficult work, really, just tedious at times. But it was oddly refreshing – I had lived such a sheltered life in that dreaded manor house – *this* was life, out here, just outside London. *This* was truly living. I had never known.

I was scrubbing the dishes for the Louvet house when the first case of plague discovered the village, about a week after our arrival. It was Cedric – Favian and Seraphina's little boy. It was my understanding that little Cedric Louvet passed it to little Josselyn and Cristiana Hendry, and then Cristiana passed it to the Hendry family household, and so on and so forth the disease took over the town. But what struck me the most was the way the villagers reacted to this sequence of happenings: the healthy celebrated life with lively song and dance, opening up casks of cedar and wine and sharing with all. The sick dropped dead suddenly and oftentimes lie where they fell, most in their beds, but many right there in the streets. The entire village seemed to have accepted its fate; determined to spend their final minutes enjoying the last of life, people drank, danced, and sang without shame or regret. For "it was a sin to try to avoid God's will," as Favian had always said. In a way, they had a point: why fight it?

But just because they accepted the inevitable fate of their forlorn village didn't mean that I had. It was time to pick up and leave again. But just as I was packing up my and Carrie's belongings, I noticed that the most important item of all was missing: Carrie. I found her in the small town's infirmary, sick with fever, and undoubtedly another causality of the ruthless plague. I collapsed at the foot of the bed, distraught with anger and fear. I stayed there watching over her for days.

Seraphina, who had become a good and kind friend to me in my village stay, saw the pain in my eyes as tended to my sister one evening. Wanting to help, she offered me the best advice she had. "Leave the sick where they be," she told me. "Save yourself." It was a valuable piece of advice, but unfortunately, one I could not take. I didn't want to leave my sister, but I didn't want to stay in the confines of this small village either with no incense to protect me, lest I expose myself to infection. I never saw her – Seraphina Louvet – again after that night. And by the time of her visit, Favian had already passed. It was no wonder she had wanted to help ease my hurt and pain.

It was Christmas season, but no one was celebrating. Those that had not yet passed still danced and drank by the firelight, but that was in celebration of life and submission to coming death: no one seemed to remember that Christmas was fast approaching and called for a different kind of celebration. I stayed with Carrie for a few days, and when I wasn't tending to her every need or comforting her with every last ounce of encouragement in my body, I found myself wondering why I had not caught the dreaded disease myself. But Carrie's needs were more dire. The course of my life ultimately resided in her survival, and I promptly dismissed the notion. I must stay strong, I resolved. If not for me, then for her. I was the only family she had left. And what I didn't want to think about: that she was mine. Until Matthias and I could be joined in matrimony, that is.

I wasn't mad. Maybe tired, but I still was aware of what was going on around me. I knew my entire family was dead in the manor house. Or, Plague House, rather. Although I did not see my parents die, I knew they were gravely ill when I left. *Moder* could barely utter her command of inspiration to me, and *Fader* was worse off than she: he couldn't even communicate by the time that I left, neither word nor action. They had all been soon to die. And all the servants had been either sick or dying. And now, weeks later, they were all gone completely – vanished as if into thin air.

But that was then. I had to focus on what lay ahead for the living.

Poor Carrie lay in silent pain and fever, covered from head to toe in dark, abnormally large abscesses. I was careful not to touch them but held her close to me just the same, remembering the physician's warnings. It seemed like a century ago. She wasn't coughing, so it didn't seem that whatever form of the disease she had was airborne. It was probably the result of her conversing and playing with the little Louvet boy, or any of the village children really. I should have exercised warnings at the very first sign of infection. But there was nothing to be done for it now. The buboes were the largest cause of her pain, and I fervently hoped against hope that there was something, anything I could do to alleviate her suffering. I prayed as usual, even more now that I was sinking into despair and needed the Lord more than ever. I gave Him thanks in this holiday season and was vaguely aware that I was the only one who did. But alas, despite my best efforts, on the eve of Christ's birth Carrie died in my arms. Her last words to me from the night before were, "Lizzie, please – please."

She had never finished the statement telling me where it hurt.

That was it, then. My entire family was deceased. I knew I must let go and move on. That was the intelligent thing to do. I had no idea what had become of Matthias, my betrothed, but all I could do now to keep myself alive was to keep moving forward. I could no longer look back lest I lose my foothold on the future and lose everything. I could not let grief for my dead family or dead sister or half-baked fantasies of Matthias hold me back. How I wished he had chosen to accompany us on our journey, but I knew I had to be selfless. I could only pray my love had done the intelligent thing and gotten away, too, just as

soon as he attended to his family. If this village was infest-
ed and breathing disease, then London, I had to imagine,
with its filthy streets and putrid air, could only be worse.

With nothing holding me back, I was now free to escape the village of Ardeley. Free to do anything I pleased.
I left that night, not stopping to pay my last respects to the
dead or say goodbye to anyone I passed along the way.
They were all too frail or morose to bother noticing me,
anyway. I traveled for months, up and down the British
Isles. I visited Oxford, Canterbury, Bristol, and York, just
to name a few. Each and every one became infected and I
escaped once again. It sometimes seemed as though I was
running from life itself. Every evening, every sunset, every
daybreak – I was on the run. It was about a year later that I
finally settled down in the city of Liverpool, which was
less hard hit than many of the others. The plague was still
raging strong, but I assumed I was far enough away from
London by now, and that was all that mattered to me. That
and my health. I was fit as a fiddle, as *Moder* would say. It
still hurt to think of her, but I had long ago let that cease to
hinder my progress. I attended religious ceremony often,
anywhere it was still in session. I devoutly believed it was
my faith that made me strong enough to continue. After
losing everything – every possession and family tie to human life I had – it was my one last constant companion. It
seemed the world was transitory – not one person I met
seemed to last. Sick, vulgar thoughts of death were these
that populated my head, I knew, but it was what I grew to
know to be a normal fact of life. People's lives were no
more sturdy than a moth-eaten wooden board, stepped on
by a young boy. They were as fragile as lilies, blowing in
the wind; as short as that of a fly; and as tenuous as the
human bond to life itself. Easily made, but just as easily
broken. If not more easily.

I had by now learned all the tricks and trade to support myself, as though I had grown up in a peasant household myself. All shreds of my vanity were long gone, left in the manor house where a part of me really did die (though I liked to believe it didn't) all those months ago. It was as if I had grown up a peasant girl and lived in her shoes my entire life. I often thought I would have been better off that way. Oh how I amused myself with tales of fantasies of being born into a different family. At least I had my imagination. I was seventeen, almost eighteen now, and found a job as a humble seamstress in the city of Liverpool. Due to the shortage of workers, there was a drastic demand for labour and a subsequent increase in wages. I decided I would make my life there.

One clear evening just before the sun was setting, I looked out into the horizon, just dreaming. I prayed to God there was a better way, that this was not the end. This was not all there was to live for. Now, I knew it was incredibly full of myself and foolhardy, but I secretly wondered in the back of my mind if He had it in *His* mind to spare me from the very beginning. Chose me out of the millions of dead to survive. Again, I knew the notion was pigheaded and rude, and I admitted it to myself. I blatantly accepted the embarrassment such thoughts brought out in me. But still, I couldn't help wonder if I was immune.

Part of my lowly job as a seamstress and dressmaker involved sometimes managing the small, modest garment shop and vending to passersby. It was Christmastime again, and the shop was adorned accordingly. We had a sharp increase in customers due to the holiday season, and the owner, a wealthy couturier by the name of Sybbyl L. Chandelier, needed me most in the shop. There I came across many faces, most of which I knew I would never see again.

I saw one in particular that caught my eye. He wa

tall and thin, with dark brown hair and piercing green eyes that strongly resembled those of my old flame, Matthias. In fact, everything about his demeanor reminded me of him. I knew my mind was paying tricks on me, but I took a closer look anyway. And sure enough, it was just another man in the crowd who just happened to resemble my former lover and groom to be. Seeming to take my curiosity in his presence as outward friendliness, he approached the clerk area, a little girl about the age of six hand-in-hand with him. I could tell at once that she was his daughter from the matching set of piercing green that decorated her irises. Here it was: further evidence that he was just another man who could not possibly be my Matty, for a child of this age was too old to be one of Matty's, even if he had settled down with another woman and begun a family. The thought greatly unsettled me, but not as much as the way the girl looked at me, seeming to stare into my soul with those bright, dangerous eyes.

She reminded me so much of Carrie that it hurt. I had been closer to her than I was with Josef, and I silently prayed that the strange, handsome man didn't have an unseen young son somewhere behind him coming from a ways down the street. I couldn't handle another close call with deceased or lost family members today.

The man seemed to be examining me as closely as I was him. I wondered if he thought me fair the way I found him handsome, like the way Matty had told me that day in the London square, a block from the physician's office. I never did get the chance to tell him I thought him a handsome fellow, I recalled with a pang of regret.

But the man in front of me continued to hold my gaze. He muttered a question about seeing one of the blouses we had on display for his wife, and I handed it to him in a daze. As our hands brushed against the material, though our fingers did not touch, his face passed so close to mine that he was close enough to kiss. I felt his warm breath against my cheek, but I did not run, did not scream, did not utter a word. Somehow I knew this man meant no harm.

He never did buy the fine material blouse, but instead purchased a small candy token for his little girl, and she coughed and coughed as she ate it. I took pity on the poor girl. She was probably choking on the candy – the pieces were awfully large.

Then they were on their way. It was no surprise to me that I never saw them again. I knew I never would.

That night I climbed into bed feeling satisfied with my day, save for a little dizzy and unsteady. I took some mint and sage for the pain and fell asleep. The next morning I awoke with a scratchy throat, rapid pulse, and scorching fever. I had seen all this before, first in Cecily then Rohesia, then Josef and my parents, then Cedric Favian, Seraphina, and little Carrie. I knew what was coming.

"It seizes me at last."

Epilogue

April 29, 1350, *Worcester, England*

Elizabeth Chauncey
Care of: Sybbyl Le Chandelier
1958 Alderson Road
Liverpool, England

Elizabeth my love,

Where are you? I heard you survived and now reside in the town of Liverpool with plans to stay indefinitely. It took me ages to learn the area of your residence. It is nearing a year and a half since I have been graced by your presence. How I have missed you! I have good news: the squire informed me that although the death toll has reached 17,000, all that have survived by this time are now immune. This means that you and I are spared by the Lord! God bless us all. I've set up a makeshift home in the city of Worcester (northwest of London and southeast of Liverpool) and am ready for you. Come find me. We will be wed by the parson and escape to the Netherlands where this dreaded disease was not as devastating to its citizens. This letter should arrive within a fortnight, and I will wait two for your response. I send to thee a million kisses, enough to pave the way to Heaven and back. I cannot wait to lay eyes on your beautiful face again.

All my love,

Matthias de Bourgueville

The Kiss of Death – Reader's Guide

Questions for Discussion:

1. As the death toll rises and the plague begins to permeate every inch of London, Elizabeth and Matthias's home, tension also rises in a parallel fashion between them. Why do you think this happens? Do you think this is due to flaws in Matthias's religious views and moral character, or is Elizabeth judging him too harshly? Moreover, is this the inevitable outcome of circumstances and individual experiences with loss, or is it just a lovers' quarrel?

2. Early in the story, Elizabeth and Matthias bicker conversationally and appear to not always get along smoothly. How is this argument, failed to be resolved by cross and pile (modern day heads or tails), differ from their later argument on the road to the physician?

3. Later, Elizabeth identifies with Matthias's pain of the loss of a brother, and they reconcile. Do you think, because of this, she is forced to "come to her senses," or is there more to it? Would this reconciliation have still happened even if Elizabeth had not lost any family members to "even the score"?

4. The story raises many questions of morals and ethics. Do you think boarding up "Plague Houses" and containing the spread of disease was a good decision in the eyes of the London councilmen? What would you do if you were in a position of power among the Medieval London government? Would you end the law? Why or why not? What would be the consequences of either action? Would you rather risk the spread of the

disease to more people in the city, or contain it and sacrifice a few to save many? What about from the perspective of those still living left trapped inside? Is either side justified? How so?

5. How would you feel if your house was deemed a "Plague House" and boarded up? Would it no longer feel like your house, and would you put distance between it and yourself as Elizabeth does?

6. Juliana's advice to Elizabeth on her deathbed marks an important turning point in the story. Do you think you would have had the strength and foresight to escape a Plague House on your own, before encouragement from your mother? If so, how and why would you go about this? If not, do you think you would have been brave enough to listen to your mother's advice?

7. What would you pack if you had to make the split-second decision to flee a Plague House?

8. The story is told mostly in the perspective of Elizabeth. How you do you think Carrie felt being dragged along by her big sister across Europe?

9. There are several themes present in the story. The plague is at the forefront of conflict, but a hint of romance soon dots the horizon as well. Matthias says that it took a tragic experience to come to terms with his love for Elizabeth. "It wasn't until I thought I would lose you that I – I realized –" If not for the unfortunate circumstance of something so immediate: life or death, would Matthias have ever uncovered his love for Elizabeth? Would they have ever gotten together?

10. At what point do you think Matthias discovers his

love for Elizabeth? Did he know it all along? Why or why not? If so, was it not yet made manifest to him, was he lying to himself and hiding the truth of what he felt, or did he purposely choose to keep it from her?

11. "If we both survive this hell, we shall be wed, regardless of what the parents say," Matthias boldly professes. Does this strong statement remind you of any other literary accounts of romantic tragedies? Use those works to draw connections to this statement.

12. "Elizabeth, if this plague has taught me nothing other than one important lesson, it is this: life is too short to not live it fully. And if this is all the time I have left to live, I'd rather spend the rest of it with you." Matthias's words of 1348 resonate strongly with ideals of today. Elizabeth echoes this sentiment: "I knew now how tenuous our lives were and to treasure every precious second I had with him." How does this connect to modern day sayings of living life to the fullest, as you only have one chance? How does this connect to your own life?

13. If you went through a tragic experience such as this which forces realizations of character among both Elizabeth and Matthias, what would you discover about yourself? What would you change? Both internally and externally?

14. Elizabeth's parting from Matthias near the bridge to the River Thames involves a huge revelation of character as the lovers come to terms with the dissonance between their feelings and the reality of their current situation. Elizabeth's view on the matter encompass the mood of the small parting bridge scene: "I didn't care who saw us there on the street or if the dead stood up in the graves to watch. If this was Hell – London and

all the death and darkness around me – then this kiss with Matthias was my small piece of Heaven." What is the significance of this, their first and only kiss?

15. If Matthias had agreed to flee the city with Elizabeth and her sister instead of staying to care for his family, would the story have turned out differently? Would you have preferred this ending? In what ways would this affect the relationship dynamics between the three of them? Would Carrie have survived? Would Elizabeth? Discuss the theoretical impact of this outcome.

16. How do you think Matthias spent his time during the year and half between their last meeting and the arrival of the letter as he searched in vain for his one true love? Discuss what you envision to be his travels across Europe.

17. Were you shocked by the letter, or do you think this was an inevitable fate in a time where people lost whole families to the dreaded disease? Did you believe everything would work out well, as in a romance story, or did you predict this unfortunate ending, a romantic tragedy echoing *Romeo and Juliet*?

18. Is this a satisfying ending? What emotional responses, if any, did it illicit in you? How do you think the author brought out these responses? What literary devices did she use to involve the reader?

19. What would you change about the ending, if anything?

20. Now, take on the role of the author and write an alternate ending.

21. If you were to continue the story, consider the follow-

ing: Does Matthias discover that the letter never arrived? Is he devastated? Is he still searching for Elizabeth? Does he cross paths with Sybbyl Le Chandelier and hear firsthand of his betrothed's death? Does he eventually settle down and make a new life for himself without her? Is he really the only one with true immunity to the plague?

22. How does the author use dialogue and description to capture the flavor of the time period? Was it effective in transporting you to Medieval London? Why?

About Sarah Natale

Sarah Natale is the author of debut book, *The Kiss of Death*, which was actually an assignment in her senior creative writing class. *The Kiss of Death* was destined to become her debut after receiving a fine arts literary award.

Sarah has been called an L.A. Gal (Language Arts Girl) due to her passion for words. She loves reading, writing, figure skating, and playing classical piano. She can be found surrounded by books with an open notebook, pen in hand. Sarah Natale, literally translated, means the Princess of Christmas.

Sarah is pursuing a double major in Creative Writing and Public Relations at Drake University. She is from the suburbs of Chicago where she is at work on her next book.

Made in the USA
Charleston, SC
06 July 2016